THE OUTFIT #6

THE STRANGE TALE OF RAGGER BILL

Robert Swindells

AWARD PUBLICAT

ISBN 978-1-78270-058-6

Illustrations by Leo Hartas

Text copyright © 1993 Robert Swindells
This edition copyright © 2014 Award Publications Limited

First published by Scholastic Ltd 1993
This edition published by Award Publications Limited 2014

Published by Award Publications Limited,
The Old Riding School, The Welbeck Estate,
Worksop, Nottinghamshire, S80 3LR

www.awardpublications.co.uk

14 1

Printed in the United Kingdom

CONTENTS

THE STRANGE TALE OF RAGGER BILL

CHAPTER 1

A SOUND GUY

It was three fifteen. School was out. A knot of small children was following a ragged, shambling figure along the high street, chanting:

"Ragger Bill, Ragger Bill,
Will he eat you?
Yes he will!"

The man walked doggedly, seeming to ignore the children's taunts, but they were taking care not to get too close.

"Ragger Bill, Ragger Bill,
Will he eat you?
Yes he will!"

The man turned so abruptly that a mane of wild red hair swung across his weather-beaten face. The children piled into one another as their leaders halted in their tracks, ready for flight. They stood squealing and giggling as the ragged man shook his fist.

"Gerraway, d'year? Thtoff thoutin' an gerroffome 'fore I thkelp ya!"

The children laughed. "Thtoff thoutin'!" they mimicked. "Thkelp ya!" But when the man took two rapid steps towards them they broke and fled.

"See that, Shaz?" growled Mickey to his companion as the infants stampeded past. "Not funny, baiting poor old Ragger. Not fair."

"Ah, come *on*," said Shaz. "*We* used to do it when we were in the infants, Mickey. Don't you remember?"

"Sure I remember. Doesn't make it right though, does it?"

"No, but..."

"He's a sound guy, old Ragger. Talks funny, but he can't help that. He roams the woods at night. I bump into him sometimes when I'm out with Raider." Mickey grinned. "He's there for the takeaway suppers, same as me."

Shaz nodded. "*Rabbit* suppers, you mean. You're a pair of poachers, aren't you? That's why you get on."

"Partly," said Mickey. "It's partly that, and partly because I take the time to listen to him.

People don't listen to Ragger because of his speech impediment. They can't tell what he says half the time and they get embarrassed."

"I know. *I* can't tell what he says."

"No, but you would if you listened regularly. You get used to it, same as anything else."

The two boys caught up with the ragged man just as he was leaving the high street to cut across the green. He stopped when Mickey hailed him.

"Hi, Bill."

"Oh – herro Mickey. 'Owth it goin', mate?"

Mickey shrugged. "School. How d'you *think* it's going?"

The man chuckled. "Never reckoned thkool mithelf. Wagged off moathtly. Whoath ya mate?"

"He's called Shaz," said Mickey. "Shazad Butt for short."

"Ro Shaz."

"Hi, Rag … I mean, Bill."

The man chuckled again. " 'Thallright – call me Ragger, lad. All the kidth do."

"I know, but…"

"I tolja – dothen marrer. Gorra go. Thee ya later, OK?"

They gazed after Ragger as he shambled across the green, heading towards the stretch of derelict land where he had his home. Ragger lived inside a rusty boiler, which had heated the school before the place converted to oil. It wasn't fancy, but it was rainproof and windproof and plenty big enough for one, and Ragger had lived in it since before the two friends were born.

"I told you," said Mickey. "Sound guy."

"Seemed OK to me," agreed Shaz. "Are we seeing the girls tonight?"

"Course we are. Seven sharp at HQ. Supposed to be dreaming up something to do at the weekend, remember?"

"I do now. See you at seven then."

"Yeah, see you Shaz." The boys separated, each heading home; each thinking about the strange wild man whose home was an old school boiler.

CHAPTER 2

ACTION

It was five past seven when Shaz arrived at Outfit HQ – the long hut in a corner of Farmer Denton's field which The Outfit used as its base. On the door was a sign:

HEADQUARTERS
THE OUTFIT
NO ADMITTANCE

Shaz pushed open the door. The other four were there already, seated around the table. They were Mickey, Jillo and Titch Denton and Mickey's dog, Raider. Raider had a basket by the iron stove, but he also had his own chair because he liked to be one of the gang. They all looked at Shaz.

11

"You're late," said Titch, who at seven was the youngest member – unless you count Raider, who was four.

"I know. Sorry. Had to go down the minimarket for Grandad." Shaz's parents were on a long visit to Pakistan and he was staying with his grandad. "Has anything been decided yet – about the weekend, I mean?"

"Yip!" said Raider.

"It has *not*, you barmy mutt," growled Mickey, "and you can get those elbows off the table."

"Something's happened, Shaz," said Jillo.

"Something serious. It's sort of put us off discussing the weekend."

Shaz looked at her. "What is it?"

"A kid's gone missing. A five-year-old girl. It was on the six o'clock news."

"You mean here, in Lenton?"

"Yeah. Me and Titch heard it on *Local Roundup*. They think she either wandered off or was taken, from outside the Infants."

"When?"

"Today. After school. We thought we'd help look for her when you arrived."

"Sorry," said Shaz again. "If I'd known..."

"Doesn't matter," put in Mickey. "What matters is getting down there and lending a hand before dark." He pulled a face. "You never know – we might look in places no one's though of, and Raider's nose could come in handy as well."

The children needed no further prompting. Chairs scraped back. Jackets were snatched from the hook behind the door. Raider fetched his leash. In ten seconds the hut was locked and empty. The Outfit was in action once again.

CHAPTER 3

MOTORMOUTH

They knew Weeping Wood best because the girls' father owned it. Mickey's caravan stood in Weeping Wood too, so that's where they went. There were nine police officers and lots of villagers. A sergeant was getting them into a straight line. He looked at the children. "Come to help, have you? Good. Join this end of the line then."

When the line was complete, the sergeant gave the order to move forward. Everybody had to go at the same slow pace, scanning the ground for anything that might be a clue. They waded through thickets and across clearings, looking and listening. Birds fled twittering at their approach. A rabbit burst from a tussock and went scuttering away with Raider in hot pursuit. They saw a vole, a stoat and two

14

squirrels, but no little girl.

The man on Mickey's right was hot. He had a big red handkerchief, and as he walked he kept mopping his forehead with it, muttering to himself all the time. Presently he said, "Wasting our time if you ask me."

Mickey glanced at him. "What d'you mean?"

"Well, it's obvious isn't it? That tramp's got her. You know – the funny fella. Forever shouting at the kids, he is. They should grab him before he does a bunk, instead of tramping about in the woods."

Mickey was about to protest when the next person in line – a woman he'd seen around the village – broke in. "I reckon you're right, George. First thing I thought when I heard. It's *him*, I says to myself. The funny fella. There's got to be something not quite right about a man who lives in a boiler."

Mickey shook his head. "He wouldn't hurt a kid, old Bill. He's not like that."

The man called George scoffed. "How do *you* know? Friend of his, are you?"

"Yes," said Mickey, "as a matter of fact I am, and I'm telling you he's harmless. Unusual, but harmless. He wouldn't hurt a fly."

"It's not a *fly* that's missing," the woman snapped. She looked at Mickey. "Aren't you the kid who lives alone in a caravan somewhere round here?"

"I live in a caravan, but not alone. My dad's there part of the time."

"Ah." George nodded. "Caravan, eh? That explains it."

"*What* does it explain?" cried Mickey.

The man smiled tightly. "Why you stick up for the tramp of course. Caravan. Boiler. Misfits, the pair of you. There ought to be a law."

Mickey made no reply. He was seething, but he didn't know what to say so he shook his head and ploughed on, and presently the line reached the end of the wood without finding anything.

"Told you," grunted George, as the sergeant called his officers together, leaving the villagers to straggle back to Lenton. "Waste of time. Tramp's probably fifty miles away by now."

"It's *not* Bill, I tell you," grated Mickey. "He's not a criminal, and he's not a tramp either. He doesn't move around. He lives in Lenton. And he works. He's a villager, same as

16

you and me."

"You?" George laughed harshly. "You're not a villager, kid. You're a flippin' gypsy or tinker or something. You want to hitch a horse to that caravan of yours and move on if you ask me."

"I *don't* ask you," snarled Mickey. "So you can keep your twisted opinions to yourself."

"What's up?" asked Jillo. The line had disintegrated. Shaz and Titch joined them.

Mickey shook his head. "It's nothing. Some motormouth sounding off, that's all." He turned away. "Raider! C'mere boy." The lurcher trotted to him, tongue lolling. "OK folks. Let's go." They turned and walked back into the wood, leaving George and the woman to gaze after them.

CHAPTER 4

A LIST OF PLACES WE KNOW

"There's loads of other places to look," said Titch, when they were back at HQ.

Jillo nodded. "Yes Titch, but it's nearly dark. The most useful thing we can do tonight is make a list of places we know, and search them tomorrow after school."

"Givenham Keep," said Titch, "*That's* a creepy enough place. Put it at the top of the list."

"Givenham Keep's a convent now, Titch," laughed Mickey. "It's the least likely place in Lenton."

"Oh, is it? I didn't know. Last I heard it was empty."

"There's that other house," suggested Shaz. "The one by the canal. That's still empty."

"Hang on," said Jillo, "we might as well

do this properly." She fished a ballpoint pen
out of one pocket and a diary out of another
and sat down. She found a blank page in her
diary and wrote HOUSE BY CANAL. She
shivered, remembering how she'd once been a
prisoner in that awful place. "Now," she said.
"Suggestions please, only one at a time. I'm
not a flipping computer."

"Sycamore Thicket."

"The old mill."

"All those dilapidated outbuildings on
Kilchaffinch Farm."

There was no shortage of suggestions. When
the children locked up at nine o'clock and went
their various ways, Jillo had a list of twenty-
six places to be searched the following evening.
"Shame it's only Friday tomorrow," said Shaz.
"If it was Saturday we'd have all day."

Mickey shrugged. "We'll have to hope we
can whizz round 'em all, won't we?"

"What we *hope*," amended Jillo, "is that the
poor kid's found safe and well in the next few
hours so we don't have to search at *all*."

"Yip!" went Raider, who was only really
keen on searches after rabbits.

CHAPTER 5
FUNNY PEOPLE

"Now, children." Mrs Latimer waited till everybody was looking at her. It was ten past three and the school week was ending. "We all know about the sad thing which happened yesterday in our village. What sad thing am I talking about, John Wallingford?"

"Miss, the little girl. Florence Inman."

"That's right. Florence walked out of this school at home time yesterday and disappeared. Nobody knows why yet, and until we do, we must all be extra careful out of doors. What must we never do, Shazad Butt?"

"Get in a car except with our mum or dad, Miss."

"What else, Jill Denton?"

"Miss, never talk to strangers or go anywhere with them, no matter what they say."

"And what else, Lindsay Pegram?"

"Never take short cuts or play in lonely places by yourself, Miss."

"That's right, Lindsay." Mrs Latimer's eyes flicked from face to solemn face. "There are funny people about. Funny people. Remember that, children, because I want to see every one of you safely back here on Monday morning. Now I fancy most of you will find a parent or other relative waiting to take you home, but if nobody's come for you, don't set off by yourself. Find somebody to walk with, and go *straight home*. No playing along the way – especially on the waste ground beyond the green. Remember what I said about funny people." She looked at her watch. "Right. Put your chairs up. *Quietly*, Richard Muff. That's better. Good afternoon, children."

"Afternoon, Miss."

Outside, Jillo looked at Shaz. "She meant Ragger Bill, didn't she?"

"Did she?"

"Course she did. *Especially on the waste ground beyond the green*. Why mention that, except Ragger lives there?"

21

Shaz nodded. "You could be right, Jillo. Seems half the village thinks Ragger took the kid. I wonder if the police have talked to him yet?"

"Bound to have. Look – Mum's brought the Range Rover. We can drop you off."

"No, it's all right."

"'T*isn't* all right, you div! You heard old Latimer. *Don't set off by yourself.* Come on."

"Oh, all right. Grandad would probably have come for me, only he doesn't walk too well these days."

They dropped Shaz by his grandad's gate.

"Thanks, Mrs Denton."

"You're welcome, Shaz. Straight inside now."

"And don't forget tonight," said Titch. "Six o'clock."

"I won't." Providing Grandad'll let me out, he thought but didn't say. He waved and grinned as the Range Rover pulled away.

CHAPTER 6

STICK TOGETHER

Mickey came out of school in time to see Shaz and the girls driven away. He was about to set off walking with Gordon Spilsbury when he heard his name called. A battered van was parked by the far kerb. Beside it, wearing jeans and a leather jacket, stood his father.

"Dad!" What the heck're you doing *here*? I thought you were somewhere Leicestershire way."

The big man nodded. "I was till this morning, when I heard on the news about this poor kid." He shrugged. "Thought I'd better come home and keep an eye on mine."

Mickey shook his head. "You didn't have to, Dad. I've got Raider. We'd have been fine."

His father pulled a face. "Maybe you would son, but I wasn't prepared to chance it so here

23

I am, and here I'll stay till they find out what happened to the kid." He nodded towards the van.

"Hop in."

"Gordon's with me, Dad. Can we give him a lift?"

"Course we can. Come on, Gordon."

On the drive home, Mickey told his father about the man called George. "Told me to hitch a horse to the caravan and move on."

"Huh!" The big man growled. "I'll move *him* on if I ever run into him. Cheeky blighter." He glanced sideways at his son. "So folks're accusing old Bill, eh?"

Mickey nodded. "Just 'cause he talks funny and lives in a boiler. 'Tisn't fair."

"Well." They drew up outside Gordon's house. "The police'll clear him so I shouldn't worry. Here y'are, Gordon – signed, sealed and delivered."

"Thanks, Mr Wilbury. See you Monday, Mickey."

"Yeah, see you, Gordon."

"So." Mickey's father steered the van on to the rough track which led to Weeping Wood. "What were you thinking of doing

tonight, son?"

"Meeting the others at HQ and searching some places we know where little Florence might be."

"Hmmm – is that a good idea d'you think, when there might be a killer about?"

"Oh, we'll be fine, Dad, honestly. There's four of us and Raider." He chuckled. "Not even a killer'd tackle four kids and a lurcher."

"Ah, well ... I dunno."

"Aw Dad – I *promised* I'd be there. We're The Outfit. We can't sit at home doing nothing with a kid missing and old Bill getting the blame."

"How d'you know the others'll show up? I can't see Farmer Denton letting the girls out, and Shaz'd have to walk all the way to the farm by himself. His grandad'll never agree to that.

Mickey grinned. "Old Shaz can always dodge his grandad. You might be right about the girls though – I hadn't thought of that, but I've got to be there in case they do get out."

"Ah, well – if you must I suppose, but keep Raider with you at all times and if you do go out, stick together."

Mickey grinned. "We always do, Dad. We're The Outfit, remember?"

CHAPTER 7

TRYING TO HELP

It was exactly six when Shaz pushed open the door, flung out his arms and went "Da-daaa!" He was on time. It was only fair the others should notice. Jillo glowered at him.

"What's up with you, you mammal?"

"Six on the dot, Jillo. I'm not late."

"Big deal."

"Oh – excuse me for *breathing*," retorted Shaz. He looked around. "You've all got faces like badgers' bums – what's up?"

"It's the girls," growled Mickey. "They're grounded. Dad warned me they would be."

"Dad? You mean your dad's *home*, Mickey?"

"Yeah. Came to look after me. Great, eh?"

Shaz looked at the sisters. "And you two're grounded?"

"Well, we can be *here*," said Titch, "But

we're not allowed any further. Means we can't search."

"Beautiful." Shaz looked at Mickey. "So what do we do?"

Mickey shrugged. "The two of *us'll* have to do it. With Raider of course." He grinned. "The girls can keep house and have the kettle on for when we get back."

"You can take a running jump at yourself," growled Jillo. "There are no housewives in The Outfit." She sighed. "You go. Me and Titch'll find something useful to do."

"You sure?"

"Well, what else can we do? It'll be dark before long. If you don't go now the job won't get done."

It started to drizzle as the two boys left HQ. They turned up their jacket collars and put their hands in their pockets. Raider wanted to check out the rabbit population, but Mickey kept him at heel where he trotted in a sulk, sniffing the wet grass.

They took a path through Weeping Wood, searching Sycamore Thicket and its Roman site before moving on towards the canal. They meant to walk along the towpath and search the creepy, abandoned house where Jillo had once been imprisoned, but when they reached the canal there were policemen on the path and a rubber dinghy on the water. A constable stopped them.

"Now then lads – where you off to, eh?"

Mickey nodded along the towpath. "There's an old house, just on there a bit. We thought..."

The policeman nodded. "I know the place. What did you think?"

"We thought we'd check it out. We're looking for the kid, you see. Florence Inman."

The officer nodded again. "So are we, sonny. So are we. What's your name?"

"Wilbury. Michael Wilbury."

"And yours?"

"Shazad Butt. The kid goes to our school so we decided..."

"You decided, did you? Do your parents know where you are?"

Shaz shook his head. "I doubt it. They're in Pakistan."

The policeman frowned. "Are you trying to be clever, lad?"

"N-no. They *are* in Pakistan."

"And how about you, Michael – your folks

in Pakistan too, are they?"

"No. My dad's at home. He knows where I am. My mum left us when I was a kid."

"Hmmm. Well. D'you know what I think? I think you'd both best scoot off home before it gets dark. *One* missing kid's bad enough. We don't need two more."

"We won't go missing," protested Mickey. "We know every inch round here, and we've got Raider to protect us. That's why Dad—"

"Never mind why Dad," interrupted the policeman. "It's possible there's a killer on the loose. This is no time for you or any kid to go poking about in empty houses, and anyway you'd be wasting your time. The place has been searched." He sighed. "Unless you think you'd do it better?"

Mickey shook his head. "It's not that. We're trying to help, that's all."

"Believe me son, the best way you can help is to go home and stay there. If the little girl is anywhere around, we'll find her." He nodded towards the wood. "Off you trot, and don't hang about. It'll be dark in half an hour."

"What about old Bill?"

The policeman frowned. "Old Bill? Who...?"

"Ragger Bill. You know. Lives in a boiler."

"Ah. *That* old Bill. What about him?"

"People're blaming him and it's not fair, just because—"

"I think you can safely leave that to us, son. We don't arrest people for living in boilers, or because they're unpopular. Now get on home and stop messing with things that don't concern you, right?"

Mickey shrugged. "Right. Come on, Shaz. Heel, Raider. G'night, officer."

"Night, lads."

CHAPTER 8

I DON'T MEAN RAGGER BILL

"So what happened?" asked Jillo. It was a quarter past eight. The four were sitting round the table with mugs of tea. Outside it was almost dark.

Mickey shrugged. "We checked out Sycamore Thicket, then set off for the empty house. The police were dragging the canal. We were stopped and sent back."

"We came by the old mill," put in Shaz. No luck though."

"Hmmm." Jillo blew into her mug. "Well, me and Titch've been thinking and making notes. It's about how the kid could've vanished from outside school. Want to hear it?"

Mickey nodded. "Sure. Fire away."

"Well, it was home time, right? Three fifteen. That means parents everywhere, collecting their kids. Broad daylight." She looked up. "You know Lenton – everybody knows everybody else. Any stranger, or strange vehicle, would stick out like a sore thumb. Somebody'd notice. So if we assume there was no stranger and no strange car, what's left?"

Shaz shook his head. "What *is* left, Jillo?"

"Local people, Shaz. Familiar vehicles. People and vehicles you'd expect to see close to school at three fifteen. Anything the slightest bit unusual, somebody would've noticed."

"So if somebody had taken Florence Inman by the hand and walked her away, they'd have noticed *that*?"

"Course, unless is was her mum, and her mum wasn't there. She was late. By the time she arrived everybody'd gone."

Mickey raised his eyebrows. "How d'you know all this, Jillo?"

"Local news. There's an update every hour."

"Right." He frowned. "So if nobody could've walked her off without being noticed, how come people're fingering Ragger Bill? He'd be spotted instantly and anyway the infants're terrified of him. They think he *eats* kids. None of 'em would go off with Ragger without kicking up a terrific din."

Jillo shrugged. "You know people, Mickey. Not a thought in their heads beyond the latest episode of *Eastenders*, some of 'em." She looked at her notes. "So – here's what we've got. One: Florence Inman *definitely* vanished right outside school at around three-fifteen. Two: there was no stranger or unfamiliar vehicle in the vicinity. Three: she wasn't *walked* off or somebody would've noticed."

Jillo paused, looking round the table. "That leaves only one possibility – that she was driven away by somebody local, in a vehicle which is often seen close to school at three fifteen."

Shaz shook his head. "So what're we talking about here? A *parent's* car? A *teacher's*? What?"

Jillo nodded. "One of those, Shaz, or one we've overlooked." She shuffled her notes together and glanced at her watch. "Titch and I have to go now. I suggest we all wrack our brains tonight on the subject of vehicles we see near school. I know it's rotten, but I think a villager took that little girl, and I *don't* mean Ragger Bill."

CHAPTER 9

DITCHWATER

A villager. A villager who isn't a teacher or a parent, but who might have a car near school at home time. Mickey thought hard all the way home but all he managed to come up with was the ice cream man. Sometimes the ice cream man waited with his van till school came out, but he wasn't there yesterday. Or was he? Mickey couldn't remember but some of the parents would. If he *was* there, the police would check him out.

"What's for supper, Dad?" One good thing about having Dad home was that for once he might not have to cook for himself. No appetizing smell hit him though, when he opened the caravan door.

His father pulled a face. "Sorry son – haven't had a minute. Busy with the police."

"They've been *here*?"

"Oh aye. Only been gone ten minutes or so."

"What did they want?"

His father shrugged. "Wanted to know where I was when the kid went missing."

"Are you a *suspect*?"

"*Everybody's* a suspect, son, till they clear themselves. I was a hundred miles away but I can't prove it, so they might not be through with me yet." He grinned. "In the meantime though, I was thinking of taking a stroll in the woods to see if there's a bit of supper hopping about. Coming?"

"You bet." Rabbit pie was Mickey's favourite.

It was dark under the trees but the drizzle had stopped. The three were padding over the wet leaf mould towards the warren when Raider stopped and growled. Father and son peered where the lurcher's muzzle pointed. Something was watching them from the shadows.

"Who's there?" growled Mickey's dad. "Show yourself or I'll loose the dog."

"Thokay." A figure stepped into a patch of starlight. "Thonly me, Jack old thon. Bill."

"Bill!" Mickey's father chuckled. "Wish you wouldn't creep about like that – enough to give a fella heart attack. How are you anyway, you old scarecrow?" He gave Bill a friendly punch on the arm.

"Been bether, Jack. Lotth bether."

"Why, what's up, mate?"

"Oh – ith thith kid. Mithin kid. Can't get no work."

"How d'you mean?"

"Nobody'll gimme *jobth* Jack. No gardenth. No carth to wath. Not even thweepin. They think I done it, thee? They thayin I took the kid. I can't get dosh for grub." He chuckled, shaking his shaggy head. "Even old lady – you know – Rorry?"

"Lolly?" Jack frowned. "What about her, Bill? Surely *she* doesn't..."

"Aye she doth, Jack. Won't gimme water no more. Won't open door, even. Drinkin' ditchwater, me. Thtarvin."

"So you're after a nice bit of coney same as us, eh?"

"Aye, but no luck, Jack. Nothin' in mi thnarth. Theemth mi luckth right out."

"Well I'll tell you what, old mate. You lend

a hand, I bet we're in rabbits up to here by eleven, then we'll have a banquet. What d'you say?"

"Thoundth terrific, Jack old thon. Leth get thtarted."

CHAPTER 10

SILLY OLD GIMMER

Saturday morning Jillo and Titch were in the village with their mother. Mrs Denton was in the hairdresser's making an appointment. The two girls were sitting on the wall outside when they saw Ragger Bill in the distance. He was doing what he usually did – popping his shaggy head round the doorways of High Street's shops, asking shopkeepers if they'd like the frontage swept or the car washed. The only difference was that today he didn't seem to be having any success. The sisters kept expecting him to disappear into somebody's shop and reappear with a broom and perhaps a bucket of water, but he didn't. He was working his way so quickly from shop to shop that he was outside the hairdresser's before their mother came out.

"Hi Bill." Jillo smiled. "Nothing doing today, huh?"

The man shook his head. "Nothin', kiddo. 'Thno uthe – I'm the whatthit – prime thuthpect, thee?"

"Prime suspect?"

"Oh aye. Gerronya way, they thay. Lookin' at me like they know I done the kid. Thawful."

Jillo was about to reply when a man across the street stopped and called out, "Gerraway from those kids, you dirty tramp!"

Ragger turned. "I ... I'm not doin' nothin', Mithter. Jus' *talking*."

The man flapped a hand at Ragger. "I'm not interested in your mumbling, you barmy old scruff – get on your way before I call the police."

"He's doing no harm," protested Jillo. "He's our friend.

The man scoffed. "Oh aye – little Florence Inman's friend too, I shouldn't wonder. You don't need enemies with friends like him."

"What's going on?" Mrs Denton had emerged from the salon. Titch pointed to the man across the street. "He's saying rotten things about Bill, Mum." Her mother looked across at him, her eyebrows raised. "Well, George Melchett – minding other people's business as usual, I suppose?"

The man spluttered. "You should be *thanking* me, Missus. Looking after your kids, I was. Warning 'em about that loony old so-and-so." He nodded towards Ragger.

"Yes, well, I'll take care of my *own* children, thank you very much, George." She treated him to an acid smile. "And if push came to shove, I think I'd rather leave them with Bill than with you."

"What...?" George Melchett's eyes bulged and his face reddened till Titch thought his head would explode. He produced a large red handkerchief and mopped his forehead. "You try to do your duty around here – your *civic* duty – and what d'you get? Insulted that's what. In the street, in front of everybody." He stuffed the handkerchief in his pocket, glared across at them and stalked off, muttering.

"Silly old gimmer," snarled Titch.

"That'll do from you, young woman," said her mother tartly. She turned to Ragger. "Have you eaten this morning, Bill?"

Bill shook his head. "Can't get no *work*,

Mithith. No thweepin."

"Never mind that. Here." She fished in her purse. Ragger shook his head violently. "No no no! *Work* Mithith. No work, no dosh – *thatth* Bill. Bill'th no beggar." He stared defiantly. "No *killer* neither."

"I know that, Bill." She sighed. "Look – call in at the farm later. There's a fence to mend. Here." She dropped some coins in Ragger's grubby hand. "An advance on your wages. Get a hot meal inside you. And take no notice of stupid people."

"Thankth, Mithith. I'll thee you later. I *will*."

"I know you will, Bill. Come along girls. Minimarket next stop."

CHAPTER 11

GOoD IDEA OR WHAT?

Mickey stood by the window, watching the distant figure of Ragger Bill as he worked on one of Farmer Denton's fences. "So at least he's eaten today?"

"Well yes," said Jillo, "and Dad'll give him some dosh when he's finished so he can eat tomorrow, but *water's* going to be the worst problem."

The boy nodded. "I know. Fancy *Lolly* turning against him. I'd have sworn she was easily the kindest person in Lenton." He smiled. "Apart from myself of course."

"Of course," sneered Titch. "Mickey *Mary Poppins* Wilbury. Why don't we lend him that?" She nodded towards the five-gallon container which stood on a battered chair by the stove. It was made of clear plastic and had

43

a red tap.

"We *could*," agreed Mickey, "but it's fantastically heavy to carry full, and we'd have to keep bringing it back for refills."

Titch shook her head. "No we wouldn't. Linda Fellgate lives near the waste ground. I bet *she'd* fill it for Ragger." Linda Fellgate was a reporter on the *Lenton Echo*, and a good friend of The Outfit.

Mickey turned. "Hey Titch," he grinned, "you're a genius." He looked at the others. "Good idea or what?"

"Great," nodded Shaz.

"Sounds OK to me," said Jillo. She looked at her watch. "Half three. I reckon I could persuade Mum to run the container down there in the Range Rover."

"Yes," nodded Titch. "And if we went with her, we could call at Linda's and ask if she'd mind filling up the container every couple of days or so."

"Shall we tell Bill then?" asked Mickey. Shaz shook his head.

"Not till we've asked Linda. She might say no."

"Will she heck. And anyway, Mrs Denton'd

probably pick it up and refill it if she did."

"No, let's wait," said Jillo. "I'll go see Mum."

"Ask her if we can *all* come," said Shaz. "The Range Rover'll take four passengers, won't it?"

"Ruff!" went Raider from his basket by the stove.

"Oh, sorry," grinned Shaz. "I mean *five* passengers, not four."

Jillo smiled. "I'll see what she says."

CHAPTER 12

HARD TO BELIEVE

"Hello Linda."

"Oh – hi kids." The reporter gazed at the container Jillo was dangling. "What's that for?"

Jillo smiled. "It's a water container. I hope you won't think we're cheeky, but we were hoping you might fill it for us."

"Fill it for you?" Linda looked puzzled. "Why – what're you going to do with it?"

"Well – it wouldn't actually be for *us*, Linda. It'd be for Ragger Bill, and he'd need it refilling every couple of days or so."

"But Bill gets his water from Lily Frodsham. Always has."

Mickey shook his head. "Not any more. She's turned against him, same as a lot of other people."

46

"*Lolly* has?" The reporter's eyebrows went up. "I find that hard to believe, Mickey. I mean, Lolly's just not *like* that." Lily Frodsham had nursed her aged parents for years and years, and now that they were dead she lived alone in their big house on the far side of the green. She was a shy, gentle person, always ready to offer help where it was needed. The villagers called her Lolly because when the school lost its crossing lady a few years ago and couldn't afford another, Lily Frodsham had stepped in to do the job for nothing and had done it ever since.

"It *is* hard to believe," nodded Mickey, "but it's true, so we wondered…"

"Sure." Linda smiled and stepped aside. "No problem. Come on in." She took the container. "This is a whopper. How'd you plan to carry it when it's full?"

"Mum's outside with the Range Rover."

"Well that's OK for this time, but Ragger…"

"He's got an old pram," said Titch. "I expect he'll wheel it in that."

Linda's kitchen tap took ages to fill the container, and when it was full it was as much as she and the children could do to lug it along the hallway and out to the vehicle. They stowed it in the back. Linda smiled at Mrs Denton. "Fancy some coffee?" The farmer's wife shook her head.

"Thanks Linda, but we'd better not. I want to drop this off at Bill's place and get the kids home for their teas."

"Another time, then." The reporter watched from her gateway as the Range Rover pulled away, then gazed across the green at Lolly's big old house. After a minute she shrugged, sighed and turned to go indoors.

CHAPTER 13

COWARDS

"Hey look – something's wrong." Titch bent forward, peering through the windscreen as the Range Rover bounced across the waste ground. Her mother glanced sideways. "What d'you mean, dear?"

"I see what she means," said Jillo, looking over her sister's shoulder. "Somebody's moved the boiler. And look – that's Bill's stuff all over the grass."

Mrs Denton brought the vehicle to a halt beside the boiler which was Ragger Bill's home. It was a rusty cylinder four metres long and one and a half metres high. At one end was the round opening Bill used as a door. This opening was only sixty centimetres across, so that if you visited Bill you had to get down on your hands and knees and crawl in like an

Eskimo into an igloo. Once inside you found yourself in a dry, windproof little house with a level floor made out of wooden pallets. The pallets were much wider than the hole, which meant that old Bill had had to take them apart and reassemble them inside. Without a window it was a bit dim but it was quite snug, and there were certainly worse places a person might live in.

They piled out of the Range Rover. You could see where the boiler was *supposed* to rest – its weight had made a shallow depression in the earth fringed with weeds and grasses which were pale from lack of sunlight. Somebody – and it must have taken several strong individuals to do it – had rocked the cylinder out of its depression and rolled it some metres across the scrubby ground, leaving a wide swathe of flattened weeds. Not content with this, the intruders had bundled the old fellow's belongings – bedding, pots and pans, broken shoes and ragged clothes – out through the hole and scattered them far and wide among the thistles, docks and nettles that thrived there. And that wasn't all. Somebody had used a spray can to scrawl the word MURDERER in scarlet paint along the boiler's length.

"Oh, how dreadful!" cried Mrs Denton. "Poor Bill. And there's nothing we can *do* really – the boiler's far too heavy for us to shift."

"We could try shoving it with the Range Rover," suggested Titch.

Her mother shook her head. "Dodgy, darling. Might do more harm than good. What we *can* do is gather up his belongings." She sighed. "What sort of people would do a thing like this?"

"Cowards," growled Mickey. "They haven't the guts to face old Bill, so they wait till he's away and come sneaking around to attack his property. A boiler can't hit back, see?"

The woman nodded. "You're probably right, Mickey. I wouldn't have thought there *were* such folk in Lenton." She shook her head. "Anyway, you four start rescuing Bill's stuff. I'll pop along to the police station and report this." She smiled. "Look at Raider sniffing about. I bet *he* knows whose handiwork this is – shame he can't talk."

CHAPTER 14

LONELY PLACES

"Wath goin' on?" The children had just finished stacking Bill's belongings when he appeared, dangling a plastic carrier. Briefly, Mickey told him how they'd come with the water and found the place vandalized. Bill shook his head. There were no tears in his eyes. "Wha' they wanna do thith for, eh? I never bothered nobody – jutht kep' to mithelf that'th all."

Mickey laid a hand on Ragger's shoulder. "I know, Bill. It's nothing you've done. It's stupid, ignorant people. Mrs Denton's gone for the police."

"Poleeth?" Bill shook his head. "Poleeth fink I *done* it, Mickey. I can tell."

"No they don't, Bill. If they thought that, you'd be in custody. Looks like they're here now anyway." The Range Rover was lurching towards them, followed by a police van. The vehicles drew up side by side. Two uniformed officers got out of the van. One of them walked slowly round the boiler. The other came up to Ragger.

"Anything missing, Bill?"

"Mithin? No. Don't fink tho."

"Damaged?"

Ragger shrugged. "Nowt to damage really, Conthtable. Cloves a bit mucky tha'th all. And mi *houth* rolled over and murderer wrote on it." He shook his shaggy head. "I'm not a murderer, Conthtable. I'm *not*."

The officer looked at him. "Nobody's saying you *are*, Bill. We're here to help you."

"Thombody *ith* thaying I am!" cried Bill. "Fella wot wrote on my *houth* thayin' it."

"Yes, OK Bill. Somebody *is* saying it, and we intend to find out who." She turned to Mickey. "There was no sign of anybody I suppose, when you got here?"

Mickey shook his head. "No. There was just Bill's stuff chucked all over the place."

"Hmmm. Shame you didn't leave everything as it was, Michael. Might have destroyed evidence, tidying up."

Mickey pulled a face. "Didn't think."

"No, well…" The officer walked over to join her partner examining the boiler. Mrs Denton, Ragger and the children stood in a knot, watching. Raider was still sniffing around. The humans thought he was sniffing for clues but he wasn't. Clues don't have long ears and fluffy tails. You can't flush them out and chase them. Raider was sniffing for rabbits.

"Don't suppose they'll catch anybody," said Mrs Denton. "Can't be many clues around in a case like this."

"There might be fingerprints," said Titch. "On some of Bill's stuff."

Her mother nodded. "There will be, darling but they're not much help unless the police can match them with the prints of a known criminal." She sighed. "Whoever did this is cruel and stupid but he's probably not a criminal."

One of the officers talked into his radio. Presently a patrol car came bouncing over the waste ground. A man in a suit got out. "Detective," whispered Jillo. The man joined the two officers and they conversed in low voices, pointing to the boiler, Ragger's belongings and the scrubby field. Presently the woman officer came over.

"Our colleague's going to dust for fingerprints," she said, "and take a sample of the paint. When he's finished we'll help you return the boiler to its original location." She looked at Bill. "I'd watch myself if I were you, Bill, over the next few days. Don't leave home unless it's absolutely necessary, and if you *have* to go out, avoid lonely places, especially if you're alone."

Ragger gazed at her. "I'm *alwayth* alone, Constable," he said.

CHAPTER 15

ALL NIGHT LONG

Sunday morning, eight o'clock. Mickey and Raider were sitting on the caravan step while Mr Wilbury cooked breakfast. It was warm for September, but the leaves were beginning to turn and the grass was drenched with dew. You could see footprints where Mickey had walked to the edge of the wood to pick mushrooms and come back again. Those mushrooms were now sizzling in the pan with eggs and bacon.

Mr Wilbury turned, spatula in hand. "I've just had a happy thought, Mickey."

"Oh yeah," said Mickey, who'd been thinking about the missing child. "What's that then?"

"Why don't I make a bacon, mushroom and egg sandwich – a really *humongous* one – and we can take it down to old Ragger?"

56

Mickey nodded. "Good idea, Dad. D'you mean this minute?"

"Naw – when we've had ours, son. Don't want to spoil the old scarecrow's Sunday morning lie-in, do we?"

When, three quarters of an hour later, the pair approached Bill's boiler, they found him trying to scrape the word *murderer* off its side with a kitchen knife. He turned quickly when he heard them coming.

"Hey up, Bill!" greeted Wilbury senior. "Bit early for you, isn't it?"

Ragger pulled a face. "No thleep latht night, Jack old thon. Not a wink."

"Why no – out rabbiting or summat?"

"No no, not that. *People*, Jack, chuckin' thtoans at the boiler. Clang, clang, every two minut'th. Hittin' it wiv thtickth too. Laughing. All night long."

"What people, Bill? Who were they?"

Ragger shook his head. "Din't *thee* 'em, Jack. Kept mi head down, but no thleep."

"They try to get inside?"

"One." Ragger chuckled. "Belted hith head wiv a mallet, I did. Didn't try it no more."

"Hmmm." Jack Wilbury frowned. "Dangerous though, my old scarecrow. What if they'd taken it into their heads to chuck petrol through the hole, and the match?"

"Ooooh, don't *thay* that, Jack!"

"Well – you can't tell with people of that sort. D'you know what I reckon?"

"What?"

"I reckon you better come kip with Mickey and me in the van till all this blows over."

"In your caravan? Ith there *room*, Jack?"

The man shrugged. "We'll make room, old son. Can't have you being harassed by thugs every night. Here." He thrust a greasy paper bag in Bill's hand. "Spot of breakfast. Get it down yer, then you and the lad start getting your stuff out while I fetch the truck. Can't leave owt here or it'll be gone. See you in a bit."

CHAPTER 16
SOMETHING RED

"We better go by Linda Fellgate's place," said Mickey as the last of Ragger's property was stowed in the truck. "Let her know you won't be needing water for a while, Bill."

They squeezed into the cab. Raider sat on Mickey's knee and pretended to drive. They bounced across the waste ground and pulled up by the reporter's gate. "Hey look," said Mickey. "That window's boarded up."

His father nodded. "Accident. Kids with a ball I bet."

"Or people," put in Ragger. "Thame people frow thtoanth at my houth."

"I'll ask," volunteered Mickey, pushing Raider out of the cab and climbing down himself. He went up the path and knocked on the door. Linda opened it. She looked tired.

"Oh, hi Linda," said Mickey. "I've just called to say old Bill won't be needing water for a while. He's moving in with us."

"With you? Why?"

"His place was attacked last night. Stones."

The reporter nodded. "So was mine, Mickey. Two a.m. Every downstairs window."

"Oh no! *Why*, Linda?"

She pulled a face. "There was a note wrapped round one of the stones. *No water for the killer*, it said."

Mickey whistled. "Have you got it – the note?"

Linda shook her head. "Police took it. I've been picking up glass since four. I'm down to the small bits."

"D'you want a hand?"

"No, no it's OK Mickey. It'll be done in no time now."

"Did they find any clues, the police?"

Linda shrugged. I don't know. They poked about in the garden but it wasn't properly light. Perhaps they'll come back."

Mickey nodded towards the boarded window. "Who fixed that?"

"A glazier the police called out. He's

supposed to be coming back this morning to fit new glass." She smiled. "I'm in for a full day."

"Yeah, well..."

"You get on, Mickey – I'm sure you've got a full day as well."

"Well yes, but it doesn't seem right to just leave you with all this. I mean, it's our fault it happened really. If we hadn't..."

The reporter shook her head. "It's not your fault at all, Mickey. You were helping a friend. You get old Bill up to your place and I'll see you later, OK?"

"OK Linda. I – I hope they catch..."

"Yes, so do I. Bye, Mickey."

He was almost back at the truck when he noticed Raider was missing. He turned. "Raider!" He could hear the dog, yipping and snarling round the side of the house. "Raider – come here you barmy mutt!" There was no immediate response, and he was about to walk back when Raider appeared with something hanging from his mouth. Something red.

"Come on, boy – fetch it." The dog bounded towards his master. Mickey plucked the animal's find from the grinning jaws and shook it out. It was a large red handkerchief.

CHAPTER 17

ARE YOU GOING TO ARREST HIM?

Mickey stuffed the handkerchief in his pocket and climbed into the truck. Raider jumped on to his knee. "You were right, Bill. Linda had a visit from your little friends too."

Ragger nodded. "*Thought* tho, Mickey. It was jutht a *feeling* I had."

"Well." Jack Wilbury chuckled. "P'raps we better move *Linda* into the van while we're at it."

"Can't though, can we?" sighed Mickey. "Will you drop me at the police station, Dad?"

"What for, son?"

"I think I might be able to help them with their inquiries."

"How?"

"With this." He produced the handkerchief.

"What is it?"

"Hanky."

"I can see that. What I mean is, where'd you get it?"

"Raider found it. In Linda's garden. It's a clue."

His father shook his head. "It's a hanky, son. It might have *blown* there."

Mickey grinned. "It might have but it didn't. Drop me off, Dad, please."

"Oh, all right son – but you're not to go bothering the police, understand? Don't get in the way. They've enough to do without that."

Sergeant Hunt was at the front desk. Mickey went up to him.

"Yes, lad?"

"I've just been at Linda Fellgate's house, Sergeant. Her windows were smashed last night."

The sergeant nodded. "We know that, son. We're investigating."

"I can help. I found a clue. Or rather my dog did."

"Oh, aye?" Sergeant Hunt looked sceptical.

"One of our detectives missed it, eh? Perhaps your dog should be on the force, lad."

Mickey nodded. "He applied but they turned him down 'cause he wears glasses."

The sergeant frowned. "We're very busy just now, son. No time for mucking about."

"I'm not mucking about, Sergeant. Look." He laid the handkerchief on the counter. The officer peered at it. "A handkerchief. So what?"

"It was in Linda Fellgate's garden."

"So – it was in the garden. It might have blown there."

"Have you been talking to my dad?"

"What?"

"Nothing. The point is, I know whose hanky this is."

"You do?" Hunt gazed at Mickey. "Whose is it, then?"

"George Melchett's."

"You don't say?" He picked up the handkerchief by a corner. "Got his initials on, has it?"

"No, but I've seen him with it. Twice."

"How d'you know it was this particular one, lad? There must be millions of red handkerchiefs."

"I *know* it's his," insisted Mickey. "He hates Bill. Are you going to arrest him?"

The sergeant laughed. "Oh, aye. I'm going to smash his front door in and say, George Melchett, I'm arresting you for hating old Bill and having a big red hanky. No." He shook his head. "Leave the handkerchief with us, son. It *might* be important, and we might want to talk to you later."

Mickey nodded. "You know where I live." He smiled. "Most of Lenton'll be living there soon anyway."

"What?"

"Nothing." He left the station and set off to walk up to HQ, where The Outfit was meeting at half-past ten.

CHAPTER 18

SOME LITTLE THING

They were waiting for him. "See the news this morning?" asked Titch. Mickey shook his head.

"The parents were on."

"What parents? What you on about, Titch?"

"The *kid's* parents, dipstick. Mr and Mrs Inman."

"It was an appeal," explained Jillo. "You know – *if you're watching and you're holding our little girl, please, please send her home.* They were both crying."

Mickey shook his head. "We were out, me and Dad. Down Ragger's place." He told them about old Bill's disturbed night and Linda Fellgate's windows. He told them about the handkerchief, too.

"So you reckon it's George Melchett causing

all the trouble?" asked Shaz.

"Oh, aye. Don't *you*?"

Shaz shrugged. "He's that sort of guy all right. You don't suppose...?"

"What?"

"You don't think *he* took the kid?"

"Oh, no! No chance. He's a big daft lump, George Melchett, but he's not like that."

"Somebody is though," said Jillo. "Somebody local. Any fresh thoughts on *that*?"

There were no fresh thoughts. Titch had filled the kettle at the house. They brewed tea and drank it. Jillo sighed. "It's grinding to a halt, our investigation. We've searched everywhere we can think of. We've wracked our brains for a suspect and we've come up with nothing. Is The Outfit slipping, d'you think?"

"Is it heck!" cried Titch. "We need a lead, that's all. Even the police are stuck for want of a lead. *Something'll* happen soon – some little thing, then we'll be away." She looked across at Raider. "Am I right, boy?"

"Yip!" said Raider.

CHAPTER 19

SSSH!

It was after midnight when Ragger Bill remembered his pipe. Mickey and his dad were asleep in snug bedrooms either end of the caravan. They'd fixed up a makeshift bed for Bill on the living room floor, but he was a poor sleeper. He was often out at night poaching, and when he wasn't he'd sometimes sit for hours on a wooden box outside his boiler, puffing on his pipe, thinking. The pipe was one of his few comforts, but in all the hassle of moving house that morning he'd forgotten it. It was with his tobacco pouch and a few small treasures in a biscuit tin right at the back of the boiler, if some snooper hadn't crawled in and nicked it.

He got up and pulled on his boots, quietly so as not to disturb his hosts. Raider, on a rug under the table, raised his head and growled.

"Sssh!" hissed Ragger. It'th OK boy. Go back to thleep."

A fine drizzle was falling. The old man closed the door, turned up the collar of his ancient jacket and hunched into it, striding rapidly into the trees and down through Weeping Wood towards the Lenton Road.

At the edge of the wood he paused, listening. The wet road glistened in front of him. There were no pedestrians, no traffic. He crossed. A line of beeches screened the waste ground from the road. He stood under these for a moment. All was silent, so he set off across the scrubby expanse of weeds and scattered rubble. Sometimes travelling folk stayed here for a few days, parking their trailers and staking out their shaggy horses, but there were none tonight. He reached the boiler and crawled inside. Its hollowness amplified the hiss and drizzle made on its rusty flank.

Nobody had been here. The few bits and pieces he'd left were undisturbed. He located the biscuit tin by touch, tucked it under his arm and crawled outside. He'd straightened up and was about to start back when he heard something and stopped dead. He cocked his head on one side and waited, but the sound wasn't repeated. After a while he muttered something, shook his head and set off back across the bumpy ground.

CHAPTER 20

DAFT OR NOT

"Sleep all right, Bill?" asked Jack Wilbury as he emerged from his poky bedroom. Bill had the door open and was sitting on the step, smoking. He shook his head.

"Not tho good, old mate. Thinking all night."

"Thinking?" Jack filled the kettle and put it to boil. "What about?"

"All thor'th. Mi boiler with murderer on it. The way people look at me thinth the kid dithappeared. A noithe I heard lath night."

"Noise? What noise? *I* never heard anything."

Bill took the pipe out of his mouth and shook his head. "Not here, Jack. Down the waitht ground. I wath fetching mi pipe."

"Ah. And what was the noise, Bill?"

"It wath like … like a kid crying."

Mickey had chosen this moment to leave

his bedroom. His heart kicked and he looked sharply at the old man. "A kid? Where was this, Bill?"

"Down the waitht ground, Mickey. Ou'thide mi boiler."

"Kids cry at night," growled Jack. "Nowt fresh about that."

"No, but you thee ... there'th only one houth anywhere *near* the boiler and tha'th Lolly'th plaith. And Lolly doesthn't have a kid."

Jack shook his head. "It must've come from farther away, Bill. Over by the green, 'praps. Sound travels a fair way at night, you know. Either that or it was an owl you heard, or a rabbit with a stoat on its tail."

"Aye, well..." Bill gazed out into the misty morning. "You're prob'ly right, Jack. I'm letting mi imagination run away with me."

The trio talked of other things over breakfast, but Mickey couldn't stop thinking about that cry in the night. He thought about it all the way to school. Shaz and the two girls were in the yard when he arrived. He led them to a quiet corner. "Listen to this," he murmured, "and tell me whether I'm going daft or not." They gathered round.

CHAPTER 21

'TISN'T FAIR

"It makes sense in some ways," said Jillo when Mickey had finished speaking. "But Lolly? It's hard to believe."

Mickey nodded. "I know, and I don't think anybody *will* believe, but it fits. You and Titch worked out that it had to be somebody local, didn't you? Somebody you'd expect to see near school at home time, with a car. We thought about teachers, parents and the ice cream man but we all forgot about Lolly. She's always near school at home time – it's her job. And she parks her car on Shiffley Road, so everybody's used to seeing it there."

"Yeah, but..." Titch frowned. "How would it work? I mean, Lolly's seeing kids across the road, right? And little Florence comes along. What does Lolly do? Abandon the crossing to take the kid into Shiffley Road? Surely everyone'd notice? And anyway, what would she say to Florence to make her get in the car?"

Mickey shrugged. "I don't know, Titch. I may be wrong about the whole thing. I mean, why would Lolly kidnap a kid anyway? All I'm saying is, it's possible. We wanted a lead. This could be it."

Shaz looked at him, "So what do we do?"

"Well." Mickey glanced towards the gateway. "It might be an idea if somebody has a good snoop round Lolly's place while she's busy here."

"You mean we wag off?" asked Titch.

Mickey shrugged. "Not *all* of us, Titch. One'll do."

"And I bet you're volunteering," she growled.

"No." Mickey shook his head. "You girls haven't been getting your fair share of this investigation, Titch. I think one of you ought to go."

"Me!" cried Titch at once. "I'll do it."

Jillo shook her head. "No you won't, Titch. You're too young. *I'll* go."

"Huh!" Titch scowled. "First I'm grounded 'cause I'm a girl, then I'm dumped for being young. 'Tisn't fair."

"Life's not fair, kiddo," chuckled Shaz. "Your turn'll come, you'll see."

"Shut your face," sulked Titch.

Mickey looked at Jillo. "OK, listen. You were sick in the night and your mum's kept you at home to see how things go. You might be in later. How does that sound?"

"Fine."

"What if I split?" muttered Titch. Her sister gazed at her.

"You're a member of The Outfit. You won't split."

"We trust you, Titch," murmured Mickey. "Outfit gotta *trust* one another or it's no good." He looked at Jillo. "Try to get right round the outside. Listen for suspicious noises and look through the windows but don't go in, even if there's a way. OK?"

Jillo nodded. "See you later." She turned and sauntered towards the gateway. The yard was full of kids and nobody paid her any attention. Presently the buzzer sounded. Kids shuffled into school. Jillo was gone.

CHAPTER 22

HMMM

Lolly's house was a mansion. Its grounds, enclosed by a high wall of yellow brick, were planted with cedars and beeches of great age and height so that it was shadowy here, even on the brightest day. Jillo shivered as she passed between the gateposts and left the sun behind. Don't know how Lolly stands it, she thought, living all alone in this place. Give me the creeps, it would.

She glanced at her watch. Ten past nine. The others would be in assembly now – except Raider. He'd be in the woods with Mickey's dad. "Wish they were here," she mumbled to herself.

She walked up the driveway. The gravel she trod was dotted with weeds and furrowed by the passage to and fro of Lolly's Micra.

The rhododendrons that lined the driveway had grown unchecked so that they overhung, dripping water which turned the gravel green. All around were signs of neglect and of decay, making sinister a place which had once been beautiful.

Jillo stopped. In front of her, a flight of wide stone steps led up to blistered double doors under a crumbling portico supported on pillars. There were six windows on the ground floor and seven upstairs. Some were covered by blinds or curtains. She stood for a while, gazing from one to another of the uncovered windows, but nothing stirred beyond their murky panes. She advanced.

There were four windows she could look through. They showed her four dim rooms. In three of them the furniture was shrouded in dust sheets. In the other she saw a green velvet suite, a large empty fireplace under a great gilded mirror and a round brass table with some magazines on it. She moved round the side of the house. More windows, mostly covered. She took a couple of quick peeps and went round the back, where she climbed three mossy steps and found herself looking through a clear door

panel into an old-fashioned kitchen. A heavy-looking table occupied the centre of the tiled floor and on it, in a cracked bread-crock, stood a child's toy windmill.

"Hmmm." Jillo's heart quickened as she stared at its bright plastic sail. She cupped her hands round her eyes to block out reflection and forced herself to take her time, studying the rest of the kitchen, but there was nothing else. She was about to move away when a door directly opposite swung open and Lolly walked in.

CHAPTER 23

BIT PATHETIC THOUGH

Jillo whirled, flung herself down the steps and pelted round the side of the house where she pulled up, listening. She was sure Lolly must have seen her. Any second now the door would be flung open and the woman would come after her. She stood, heart pounding, poised for flight. Nothing happened. After a moment she flattened herself against the house and peeped round the corner. The door was still closed. Nothing stirred. By some miracle, Lolly hadn't spotted her.

What now, though? Prowling around an empty house was one thing. Creeping about with the occupant at home was quite another. Maybe she should quit and go back to school. Tell the others about the windmill.

Bit pathetic though, wasn't it? *What*

happened, Jillo? What did you find out? Oh, I saw a kid's windmill. *Yes, but did you see a kid?* Well no – I ran away actually.

No. It wouldn't do. The boys'd think, *huh – should've gone ourselves.* So.

Slowly, carefully she slid round the corner and inched back towards the steps, watching the door all the time. When she came to a window she ducked in case Lolly saw her from inside. Climbing the three steps again was worst. What if Lolly *had* seen her and was waiting behind the door? What if it flew open just as she reached the top? What if, what if, what if...

At the top she held her breath, edged forward and peeped through the clear glass panel. The door Lolly had entered by was open, but the kitchen was empty. Two laden carriers stood on the table beside the bread-crock. The woman had been carrying these when she'd come through the door. Surely she'd be back any moment to unpack them, then there might be another clue. There could be stuff in those carriers grown-ups don't use: toys or jelly babies or little white socks. *That'd* settle matters, wouldn't it? *That'd* be something to report. She waited, spooking herself by playing a little film inside her head. In the film she was waiting for Lolly to come back into the kitchen and unpack the carriers, but instead Lolly had let herself out the front door and was creeping round the side of the house. She was there now, just out of sight round the corner. The moment Jillo looked away she'd come with incredible speed and grab her because that's what Lolly *really* was – The Lenton Child Grabber. It was definitely the wrong film to be watching right now. Jillo shook her head to stop it and as she did so Lolly came back into the kitchen leading little Florence Inman by the hand.

CHAPTER 24
PREPOSTEROUS STORIES

There was no danger of Lolly seeing her this time. She was too busy smiling down at the little girl and talking to her. Jillo moved away from the door and down the steps, her heart racing with a mixture of joy and uncertainty. She'd found the missing kid and that was terrific, but what now? She was supposed to go back to school – report to the others – but that was daft now that she'd actually *seen* the child. It was too important. Too urgent. Not that the kid was in any danger – you could see from the woman's face she intended no harm, but still. She'd have to go to the police, wouldn't she?

Jillo retraced her steps around the house. Lolly's Micra was parked out front. She skirted it and walked quickly down the driveway, glancing back from time to time.

It's rotten, she thought. Poor Lolly's going to get into terrible trouble, but what can I do? Little Florence isn't *hers*. The kid's got a mum and dad and they're frantic. The sooner she's back with them, the better. Better for her. Better for them. Better for Ragger. That George Melchett'll have to eat his words now, won't he? Not fun for Lolly though. Wonder why she did it?

The police station was in the middle of the village. Jillo got there at ten past ten. Constable Pilsbury was at the counter. He was six feet ten inches tall. He gazed down at her. "Shouldn't you be in school, young woman?"

Jillo nodded. "Yes, but you see..."

"Never pass your exams, get a decent job if you wag off school, you know. What's up: off sick or something?"

"No. Well yes, sort of. I – I had to go somewhere. Do something,"

"Oh, aye?" He arched his brow. "Mum and Dad know about it, do they – this thing you had to do?"

"No-no, they don't. It was – uh– Outfit business, you see."

"Ah! *Outfit* business, was it? Now where

have I heard *that* before?"

"I dunno, but I know where Florence Inman is."

"Oh you do, do you?" He bent over the counter till his face was close to hers and spoke softly. "And where would that be, then?"

"She's at Lolly's house."

"Lolly? You mean Lily Frodsham?"

"Yes."

The constable's face came even closer. He whispered. "Are you telling me that Lily Frodsham abducted that child?"

"Yes."

"Rubbish!" He straightened up and spoke loudly. "Ms Frodsham's the most highly-respected woman in Lenton. You're letting your imagination run away with you – er – what *is* your name?"

"Jill. Jill Denton."

"Oh, aye. I remember now. Denton Farm." He stared down at her. "Well, Jill Denton, I'll tell you what I think, shall I?" He didn't wait for an answer but went on, "I think you'd better run along to school this minute and attend to your lessons, 'stead of prying into things that don't concern you and dreaming up preposterous stories about respectable folk."

"But..."

"No buts. I'll count to three, and if I can still see you I'll give your father a call. One..."

Jillo fled.

CHAPTER 25

READY TO SPRINT

"Feeling better now, Jill?"

"Yes, Miss." It was a lie. Jillo felt awful. She needed to speak to the others, but no chance right now. Wonder what Lolly's doing, she thought. And little Florence.

I could go to the head. Surely *she'd* believe me? P'raps not though – she and Lolly are close friends. Hang on till break – talk to the others.

It felt like forever but it rolled around at last. She took them for a walk on the playing field and told them what she'd seen.

Mickey whistled. "So we've *found* her." He grinned. "The Outfit strikes again."

"Yes, but what's the point if nobody'll believe us?" cried Titch.

"I vote we go straight to the kid's parents," said Shaz. "They'll be down Lolly's place like a shot, I'll bet."

"Yes, or there's Linda Fellgate," suggested Jillo.

"How about," murmured Mickey, "how about leaving it till twelve when Lolly's on the crossing and rescuing the kid ourselves?"

"I thought of that," said Jillo, "but it didn't seem right to let Mr and Mrs Inman go on fretting."

Mickey pulled a face. "No, it isn't right, but if nobody believes us, what choice do we have?" He looked at his watch. "We're only talking about one and a quarter hours, and you said yourself the kid seemed perfectly happy with Lolly."

"Yes, but..."

"Mickey's right," nodded Shaz. "An hour and a quarter's neither here nor there. I say snatch the kid at twelve."

"How do we get in?" asked Titch.

Mickey shrugged. "I dunno, do I? We'll find a way when the time comes, Titch. Just make sure you're ready to sprint when that buzzer goes. *All* of you."

CHAPTER 26

CLEAN 'IM UP A BIT

"Y'know, I can't thtop thinking about that *thound*, Jack." Mickey's dad had the rugs up and was sweeping out the caravan. Ragger was sitting outside on a wooden box, peeling potatoes.

"Sound?"

"Yeth, you know – that cry. The more I think about it, the more I'm sure it came from Lolly'th houth."

"Nah!" Jack shook his head. "Can't have, old son. Not Lolly, I told you – sound travels a long way at night."

"I *know* tha'th what you thay," said Ragger, "but I thill can't thtop thinking about it." He stood up. "I'th no uthe – I've gotta go down there, thnoop about, thet mi mind at retht."

The other man shook his head. "I wouldn't

if I were you, Bill. You know what the police said – *don't leave home unless it's absolutely necessary.* Folks're in an ugly mood over that kid, and some of 'em have got it in for you."

"Thtill gotta go, Jack."

"Yeah, well watch yourself, you stubborn old scarecrow."

He'd meant to head straight for Lolly's house, but by the time he reached the Lenton Road he'd changed his mind. *Avoid lonely places,* the police had said, and Lolly's house was certainly in a lonely place. He wouldn't go there, he'd go to the police station. Tell *them* about the cry in the night.

He turned right and walked towards the centre of the village. He was opposite the green when somebody hailed him from the car park of the Ram. The Ram was Lenton's only pub. Ragger looked across. Six or seven men were sitting on a bench, drinking beer. One of them was George Melchett.

"Five to twelve," bellowed George. "Off to school, are you, looking for another kid to snatch?"

Bill moved on without answering. He was

hoping they'd let him go but George got up and shouted, "HEY YOU – TRAMP – DON'T WALK AWAY WHEN I'M TALKING TO YOU!"

Bill looked across at them. They were all on their feet now.

"Not off to thkool," he called. "Poleeth. Thummat to tell 'em."

"Aye." George Melchett nodded. "We *know* you've summat to tell 'em, sunshine, and we know what it is and all." He looked at his companions. "Don't we, lads?"

The men nodded, mumbling. George looked across at Ragger and said, "I think he should tell us first, don't you?" His companions nodded again. One laughed, setting down his tankard on the bench.

"Come on lads," he cried. "Let's get him, chuck him in the pond."

"Yeah!" growled George. "*That's* the ticket – clean 'im up a bit."

They crossed the road, starting to run. Bill put on a spurt, hoping to reach the police station before they got to him but it was no use. They were younger and faster. Their footfalls thudded closer and he felt his collar grabbed.

Rough hands seized him and he was half dragged, half carried across the road and on to the green. Before him was the village pond, deep and dark. Bill couldn't swim. He kicked and writhed but they shoved him forward as the clock on the village hall struck twelve.

CHAPTER 27

THE WAIL OF A FRIGHTENED CHILD

They were off before the buzzer stopped, pelting across Shiffley Road, where Lolly's Micra was parked, and along Back Green Lane. Something seemed to be happening over by the pond but they didn't have time to look. They were swerving through Lolly's gateway in a shower of gravel at two minutes past twelve.

"Where now?" panted Mickey as they reached the house. Jillo shrugged. "Kitchen's round the back. You can see inside but you can't *get* in."

"Let's try the doors," said Shaz. "You never know." He ran up the steps, grabbed the big brass knob and tried to turn it. The door was locked.

"Quick!" gasped Jillo. "Round the back."
They ran round to the kitchen steps but that
door was locked, too. Jillo squinted through
the panel. The crock was on the table but the
windmill had gone.

"What do we do now?" asked Titch, "smash
the glass?"

"No." Mickey shook his head. "Not unless
we have to." He glanced at his watch. Five past
twelve. "We've got fifteen minutes at least.
Look for an open window."

They circled the house. At the far end,
where trees and shrubs crowded right up to the
house they found a dilapidated conservatory.
Its wooden framework had once been white,
but the ancient paint had flaked and blistered
and the exposed timber was split and turning
green. The myriad panes of glass were dull and
streaked with dirt. Many panes were cracked.
In a dark corner where the conservatory joined
the house, Jillo found a frame which had
lost its glass. She called the others, and one
by one they wriggled through till the four of
them stood on the conservatory's mossy brick
floor. As expected, the door that connected the
conservatory to the house was locked, but it

was flimsy compared to the two outside doors. When Mickey tried it, it rattled in its frame.

"I bet we can smash this easy," he cried. "Come on." They gathered themselves and, on Mickey's count of three, charged the door. It flew open with a splintering crash. The four children tumbled through off balance and sprawled in a tangle of arms and legs on the tiled floor of a passageway. Their arrival had been a loud one and as its echo died, they heard the wail of a frightened child.

CHAPTER 28

THE DISTURBANCE IS OVER

Lolly was a very unhappy woman. Oh, she smiled and chatted with the children as usual as she shepherded them across the road, but inside she was crying. What have I done? She asked herself over and over. What have I done, and how can I make it better? What's going to become of me when everybody knows?

She'd always meant to give the child back. She had. She'd wanted someone to care for, that's all. Just for a little while. Something to love. And she'd taken good care of little Florence. The child wasn't unhappy, except perhaps when Lolly had to leave her in her room with the door locked so that she could come to work. She'd always known Florence would have to be given back, but she hadn't really thought about what would happen then.

The police. Being arrested. Going to prison.

It doesn't matter, she told herself as she planted her lollipop in the middle of the crossing and waved the children on. It doesn't matter how frightened you are, Lily. You've been a silly old woman – a *cruel* old woman – and you'll be punished. You *deserve* to be punished. You must take little Florence home today – no more putting it off. You must take her home, apologize to Mr and Mrs Inman and take whatever comes. And whatever they do to you, it won't hurt nearly as much as saying goodbye to the child.

She was thinking these heavy thoughts when she noticed some sort of disturbance on the green. She guided the last child safely across, then walked to the kerb and screwed up her eyes. There were some men by the pond, jeering and laughing. She recognized George Melchett. On the grass at the men's feet lay another who seemed to have been in the water. At first Lolly thought she was witnessing a rescue – somebody had fallen in the pond and those men had pulled him out – but then she saw one of them draw back his foot and kick the fallen man. It was then she realized who the man was, and why this was happening.

"Stop!" Lolly was a kind, gentle person, but she was brave as well. She knew Ragger was suffering because of her, and she didn't hesitate. Brandishing her lollipop she charged across the green. "Stop!" she cried. "Leave him alone, you bullies. He's not guilty. – *I* am!"

There – it was out. The men turned as she bore down on them, her luminous jacket flapping. George Melchett bellowed, "Clear off woman and mind your own ... aaaagh!" The lollipop slapped the side of his head. He reeled, seeing stars, and plunged with a mighty splash into the pond. The others ducked and dodged, shielding their heads with their arms as the furious Lolly laid about her lustily with her black and yellow sign. Ragger, half-drowned, lay gasping as his assailants broke and ran.

Lolly, victorious, dropped her weapon and stood panting as the bullies scattered. George Melchett was hauling himself on to dry land when a patrol car came bouncing across the green. It pulled up by the pond and Constable Pilsbury got out. He gazed at the spluttering George.

"Just the man I was looking for," he said. "I believe this is yours." George Melchett clawed mud from his eyes and saw the policeman was holding up a large red handkerchief. He groaned. The lanky officer glanced down at Ragger Bill, then turned to Lolly. "What's going on?" he demanded. "There are reports of a disturbance."

Lolly's smile was tired. "The disturbance is over, Constable," she murmured, "but there's another matter you might like to deal with. Look behind you."

The officer turned. Five children were approaching. Four he recognized vaguely as a gang that called itself The Outfit. The fifth he recognized far more easily because her photograph was plastered all over the police station. Her name was Florence Inman.

CHAPTER 29
NOT IF YOU'RE A RABBIT

A chill, misty Saturday in October. In Weeping Wood leaves were falling. On Lenton high street a ragged figure moved across the frontage of a greengrocer's shop, sweeping. Inside Outfit HQ, four children and a dog sat sipping hot tea and admiring a glossy photograph pinned to the wall. It was a press photo of the Inman family, reunited and smiling. In front of the Inmans, grinning into the camera, sat Ragger Bill and The Outfit.

Jillo smiled. "Looks good."

Mickey nodded. "Course it does – it's got *me* in it."

"Huh!" scoffed Titch. "*Spoils* it, that does."

"Wonder what poor Lolly's doing right now?" murmured Shaz. Jillo looked at him. "She's resting, Shaz. That place they sent her

100

to – it's not a prison. It's a hospital for people who need a long rest. I heard Mum and Dad talking about it. Lolly looked after her parents for years and years, you see. Wore herself out. After they died she got terribly lonely, all by herself in that big old house. It made her ill. You know – in her mind. And when Florence's mum was late that afternoon, and little Florence was left all alone at the school gate, Lolly took her. Florence thought she was going to get a lift home, but Lolly took the kid to *her* place. *Borrowed* her, she said, but of course you can't borrow someone's kid. Mum says she's lucky the Inmans spoke up for her in court, and that she had an understanding judge."

Shaz grinned. "Luckier than George Melchett, anyway."

"Oh, yes. Poor old George. Three months for smashing Linda Fellgate's windows, and six months for chucking Ragger Dill in the pond. I bet he'll be a lot quieter when they let him out."

"And what *about* Ragger?" cried Titch. "They offer him a smart bungalow – one of the old folks' bungalows on Green Lane – and he says no thanks and goes back to his boiler."

Mickey nodded. "Good for him, I say. Everyone should live the way they want to, providing they're not hurting anybody else. Ragger's harmless enough, isn't he?"

Titch grinned. "Not if you're a rabbit."

"Ah, well." Mickey ruffled Raider's ears. "You could say the same about *this* guy, right?"

"Tell you what," said Titch. "It seems ages since we did…"

"THE OATH!" cried the others in unison. Titch blushed.

"I agree with Titch," nodded Shaz. "Come on."

They pushed back their chairs. Raider jumped down from his. They squatted in a circle, the dog in the middle.

"Faithful, fearless, full of fun," they chanted. "Winter, summer, rain or sun, "One for five and five for one – "THE OUTFIT!"

On the last word they leapt in the air with their arms raised, breaking the circle. "Yip!" went Raider. It was time to look for a new adventure.

READ ALL OF THE OUTFIT'S THRILLING ADVENTURES!

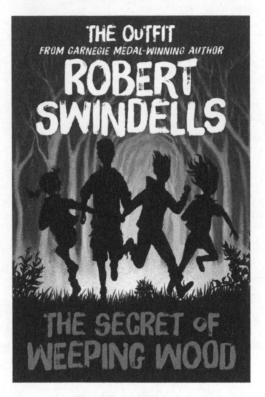

ISBN 978-1-78270-053-1

The Outfit had never really believed
the stories about the ghosts of Weeping
Wood – until now. But as they investigate
the mysterious cries, truth suddenly
becomes stranger – and more
terrifying – than fiction!

Borrowed items 09/02/2017 13:38
XXXXXXXXXX0727

Item Title	Due Date
* Algy's amazing adventures in the jungle / [paperback]	02/03/2017
* Poppy the pirate dog's new shipmate / [paperback]	02/03/2017
* The strange tale of Ragger Bill	02/03/2017
* Zombies! / [paperback]	07/03/2017
* Batpants! [	

Amount outstanding: £1.50

* Indicates items borrowed today
Thankyou for using self service

READ ALL OF THE OUTFIT'S THRILLING ADVENTURES!

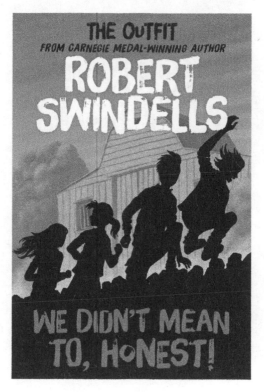

ISBN 978-1-78270-051-8

Miserable Reuben Kilchaffinch is going
to fill in Froglet Pond, and he won't let
anything, or anyone, get in his way.
The Outfit are desperate to save the pond
and its wildlife and they plan to stop
Kilchaffinch – at any cost!

READ ALL OF THE OUTFIT'S THRILLING ADVENTURES!

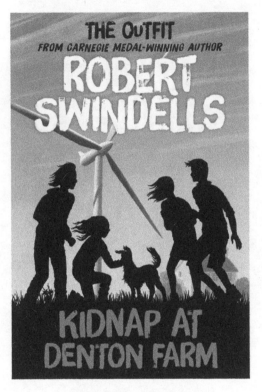

ISBN 978-1-78270-055-5

When Farmer Denton has a wind turbine built on his farm, little does he know what trouble it will bring. After one of them goes missing, The Outfit must solve the mystery of the malicious caller – and fast – if they ever want to see their friend again!

READ ALL OF THE OUTFIT'S THRILLING ADVENTURES!

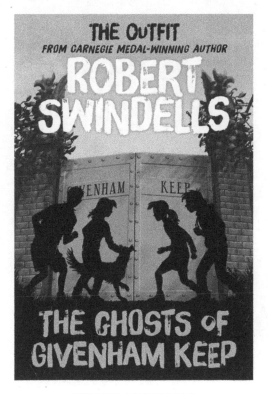

THE OUTFIT
FROM CARNEGIE MEDAL-WINNING AUTHOR
ROBERT SWINDELLS

THE GHOSTS OF GIVENHAM KEEP

ISBN 978-1-78270-056-2

Steel gates and barbed wire have
been put up around the old mansion in
Weeping Wood. Someone has something to
hide and The Outfit intend to find out what.
But their innocent investigation soon
takes a sinister turn...